Karen's Ghost

Also in the Babysitters Little Sister series:

Look out for:

Karen's Ghost

Ann M. Martin

Illustrations by Susan Tang

Hippo

Scholastic Children's Books,
Scholastic Publications Ltd,
7-9 Pratt Street, London NW1 0AE, UK

Scholastic Inc.,
730 Broadway, New York, NY 10003, USA

Scholastic Canada Ltd,
123 Newkirk Road, Richmond Hill,
Ontario L4C 3G5, Canada

Ashton Scholastic Pty Ltd,
P O Box 579, Gosford, New South Wales,
Australia

Ashton Scholastic Ltd,
Private Bag 1, Penrose, Auckland,
New Zealand

First published in the USA by Scholastic Inc., 1990
First published in the UK by Scholastic Publications Ltd, 1993

Text copyright © Ann M. Martin 1990

ISBN 0 590 55239 2

BABYSITTERS LITTLE SISTER is a trademark of Scholastic Inc.

Typeset by A.J. Latham Ltd, Dunstable, Beds
Printed by Cox & Wyman Ltd, Reading, Berks

10 9 8 7 6 5 4 3 2 1

For Paula

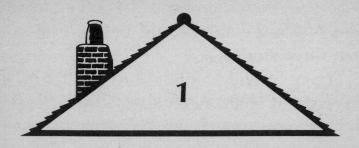

Witches and Ghosts

"Kristy, do I really have to go to sleep now?" I asked my big sister.

"Yes, you do. It's already past your bedtime."

I sighed. Kristy is one of my favourite people in the whole wide world. But she *is* thirteen. And when she says to do something, you have to do it. Besides, Kristy was my babysitter that night. And you have to listen to babysitters, just like you have to listen to teachers and mummies and daddies and grandparents and policemen.

"One more story?" I begged.

Kristy shook her head. "You've already had one more story. And before that you had three stories."

"Yeah," I said, smiling. "And all of them were about Hallowe'en."

"Are you going to be able to sleep tonight?" Kristy asked me.

"Of course," I replied. "Witches and ghosts don't scare me." (That was easy to say when the light was on and Kristy was sitting next to me.)

"All right," said Kristy. She sounded a little uncertain. "Under the covers, then. I hope you have good dreams tonight."

Kristy stood up, and I slid under my covers. I scrunched up my pillow.

"Don't forget to turn on my nightlight," I said.

Kristy switched on my special light from Disney World. Then she kissed me good night, turned off my lamp, and headed for the door.

"Leave the door open a crack!" I called.

"Okay." Kristy left my room.

I was alone.

I looked around. I was glad the nightlight was on and the door was open.

Hallowe'en was coming. That was why I wanted to hear all the Hallowe'en stories. I just love Hallowe'en. I love ghosts and witches, too. But I'll tell you something. They *do* scare me a little bit. But that's only because a real witch lives next door. And a ghost lives upstairs and haunts his room on the second floor of our house. He haunts the attic, too.

The witch is called Morbidda Destiny. Well, that's what *I* call her. It's her witch name. Most people call her Mrs Porter, but they don't know anything. Morbidda Destiny holds witch meetings at her house. At night, she flies around on a broomstick. (Adults don't believe this.)

I sat up and looked out of my window. Morbidda Destiny's broomstick was leaning by her front door. I could see it by the porch light. I decided she wasn't going to go out haunting that night.

I lay down again. I listened.

CREEEEAK. What was that? Was it Ben Brewer?

I felt pretty scared. Ben Brewer is the ghost in my house. I'm not sure if he ever drifts below the second floor. What if he does? What if he was in my room *right then* . . . watching me?

"Go away, Ben Brewer," I whispered. "You can't scare me."

CREEEEAK.

"Honest," I said. "You can't scare me." But my voice was shaking.

I sat up and looked out of the window again. Morbidda Destiny's porch light was off! Was her broom still there? Was she out haunting?

I almost called for Kristy. Then I remembered that I'd told her that witches and ghosts don't scare me.

I tried to think about other things. First I thought about Kristy. She's not really my sister. She's my *step*sister. That's because my daddy married her mummy. You see, I have two families. . . .

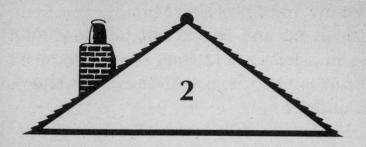

Big and Little

I think I'm lucky to have two families. Most people just have one. Some people don't have any at all. That's so, so sad.

I'm Karen Brewer. I've just turned seven years old. I have blonde hair and blue eyes and some freckles. I wear glasses. I even have two pairs. One pair is for reading and the other pair is for the rest of the time. (Well, I don't have to wear glasses in bed at night. But I have to put them on when I get up in the morning.)

I have a little brother. His name is

Andrew. He's almost five. Most of the time, Andrew and I live with Mummy and Seth. Seth is our stepfather. Mummy and Seth live in a little house. Seth has a dog called Midgie and a cat called Rocky. I have a rat called Emily Junior. Seth's a very nice stepfather.

But Andrew and I have another house and another family. That is the big house (a mansion) where Daddy lives. A long time ago, when I was still at nursery school, Mummy and Daddy got divorced. Later, they both got married again. Mummy married Seth, and Daddy married Elizabeth. Elizabeth is my stepmother. It's a good thing Daddy has such a big house because Elizabeth has four children. They are Charlie and Sam, who are at high school; David Michael, who is seven like me; and Kristy. Sam, Charlie, and David Michael are my stepbrothers. Kristy is my stepsister.

Guess what? I also have an adopted sister. Daddy and Elizabeth adopted her. She came all the way from a country called Vietnam.

She's just two years old. We named her Emily Michelle. And I called my rat after her.

One more person lives at the big house. That is Nannie, Elizabeth's mother. She looks after Emily Michelle while Daddy and Elizabeth are at work and everyone else is at school. Doesn't Daddy have a big family? It's even bigger when Andrew and I come and stay. We live at Daddy's every other weekend and for two weeks during the summer.

Oh, there are also two pets at the big house. One is Shannon, David Michael's puppy. The other is Boo-Boo, Daddy's fat old cat. I have never liked Boo-Boo very much. He scratches you if you're not careful.

The big house is the one with the witch next door and the ghost upstairs. It's a scary place around Hallowe'en. Even so, I'm glad I have two houses and two families. It's fun. Andrew and I have two of almost everything. We each have two bicycles, one at the little house and one at the big house.

I have two soft toy cats, one at each house. I even have a piece of Tickly, my special blanket, at each house. Also, Andrew and I have clothes and toys and almost everything at each house. That way, we hardly have to pack when we go back and forth between Mummy's and Daddy's.

Since we have two of so many things, I call myself Karen Two-Two and I call my brother Andrew Two-Two. Those names came from a book that Miss Colman read to our class. It was called *Jacob Two-Two Meets the Hooded Fang*. (Miss Colman is my second-grade teacher at Stoneybrook Academy.)

Oh. I almost forgot. I even have two best friends. Hannie Papadakis is my big-house best friend. She lives across the street from Daddy and one house down. Nancy Dawes is my little-house best friend. She lives next door to Mummy. Hannie and Nancy and I call ourselves the Three Musketeers. We're all in Miss Colman's class.

Being a two-two is pretty okay, I thought, as my eyes started to close.

I forgot about witches and ghosts, and fell asleep.

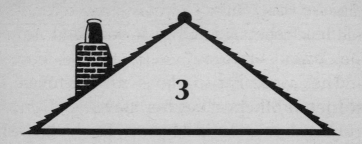

Hallowe'en

By the next morning I had forgotten about Morbidda Destiny and Ben Brewer. Almost. What I was thinking about was Hallowe'en.

As soon as breakfast was over, I said to David Michael and Andrew, "Let's plan our Hallowe'en costumes."

"Okay," said the boys.

We went to the playroom, where we have lots of dressing-up clothes.

Emily Michelle followed us.

"Go away, Emily," said David Michael. "Hallowe'en is for big kids. You're too little."

I could tell that Emily hadn't understood him.

"Play," she said. Only it sounded more like "pway" or "pray".

"She just wants to play with the toys," I told my brothers. "Let her stay."

"Okay," said David Michael. But he looked as if he thought it was a bad idea.

My brothers and I began to pull things out of the dressing-up box. We found some pretty good things. Daddy buys us costumes sometimes. He knows we like to pretend. We found hats and an Indian head-dress and a wand and a tiara and a cowboy suit and fireman's boots and more.

"I'm going to be a cowboy," said Andrew, after he'd looked at everything.

"I don't think the cowboy suit fits you," I told him. "It's too big."

Andrew tried the trousers on and they slid right off.

"Maybe next year," I said. "Next year you can be a cowboy."

"Yeah," replied Andrew sadly.

"Hey, I know! I'm going to be a Teenage Mutant Hero Turtle!" cried David Michael. "Just like on TV."

"We don't have a Teenage Mutant Hero Turtle costume," I pointed out.

"Maybe Mum will help me make one," said David Michael. "What about you, Karen? What do you want to be?"

I looked at all the stuff we had tossed on the floor. "Usually I dress up as a witch," I said. "Maybe I should be something different this year. Maybe a beauty queen or a princess. Or Raggedy Ann. That might be fun."

"Me! Yook!" cried Emily suddenly.

My brothers and I hadn't been paying any attention to Emily. When we looked at her, we saw that she'd put on high heels, a big straw hat, a feather boa, and a tutu. We couldn't help laughing a little.

Then Emily laughed, too. "Funny!" she said.

"You know, she does look pretty cute," said David Michael.

"Yeah," agreed Andrew and I.

"Maybe," said David Michael slowly, "if we get a costume for her and bring her along with us when we trick-or-treat, people will give us more sweets."

"Yeah!" exclaimed Andrew and I.

But then I stopped and thought of something. "You know," I said at last, "Emily is only two. Well, two and a half. She doesn't understand about Hallowe'en. She's too little. Just like you said, David Michael."

"Oh, forget that. That was before I saw Emily dressed up. Now, what should her costume be?" he wondered.

"Maybe *she* could be a witch this year," I suggested.

"Nah. She has to be cute," said David Michael.

"A princess?" suggested Andrew.

David Michael nodded slowly. "Yes. . . . I think a princess would be perfect. Now, what about us?"

We just couldn't decide. And we still

hadn't decided by the time Hannie Papadakis phoned and invited me over to her house.

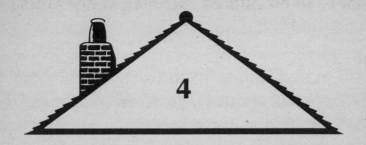

Old Ben Brewer

I went over to Hannie's after lunch. I'm always careful when I cross the road. I look both ways and make sure no cars are coming. I do that before I even step off the curb. Then I run to Hannie's.

When I rang the Papadakises' bell, Linny answered the door. He's Hannie's big brother. He and David Michael are friends.

"Hannie!" he yelled. "Your Musketeer is here!"

Ever since Linny found out that Hannie

and Nancy and I are the Three Musketeers, that is all he calls us. He's a pain.

"Karen!" Hannie called. "Come on upstairs."

I ignored Linny. I ran to Hannie's room.

"Let's talk about Hallowe'en costumes," I said, as soon as I got there.

"*I* already know what I'm going to be," said Hannie. "I'm going to be a bride. I'm going to wear my wedding dress from when I married Scott Hsu."

(Hannie is the only second-grader I know who's married. She had a wedding not long ago. She wore her mother's wedding dress and she married Scott, a boy down the street. I was the bridesmaid.)

"I don't know what my costume will be," I said. "I don't think I'll dress up as a witch again."

"How about a cat?" suggested Hannie.

I shook my head

"A rat? You could be Emily Junior."

I shook my head.

Then we both thought for a while.

"I know!" I cried. "I'll dress up as Old Ben Brewer. As his ghost."

"But then you'd just wear an ordinary old ghost costume," said Hannie. "That isn't special."

"It will be to me. *I'll* know that *I'm* Ben Brewer."

"Tell me about Ben Brewer again," said

Hannie. "Put all your stories together into one big story."

"Okay," I replied. "I'll tell you as much as I know."

I drew in a deep breath. "Old Ben Brewer was as mad as anything," I began. "He ate fried dandelions —"

"And he never left the house," added Hannie.

"Right," I said. "Well, that was when he was old. When he was young, he was just like everybody else. He got married, and he and his wife had a son, Jeremy. Jeremy was my grandfather, only I never knew him. He died before I was born.

"Anyway, when Ben was an old man and he was living alone in our big house, a ghost began to haunt him. He would come to Ben's bedroom at midnight. Ben did everything he could to keep the ghost away, but the ghost always got in. You know how ghosts are. The ghost would come down the chimney or even walk right through a wall or the door. There was no way to escape that ghost." (I had heard bits and pieces of the rest of this story from Daddy and other people.)

"Why did the ghost haunt Ben?" asked Hannie.

"I don't know," I replied.

"And how did Ben Brewer become a ghost himself?"

"I don't know that, either."

Hannie looked disappointed. We began talking about our Hallowe'en costumes again.

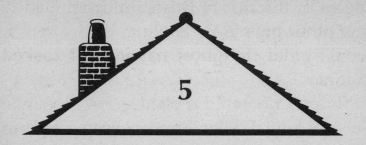

Scary Stories

Miss Colman is the best teacher I've ever had. For one thing, she hardly ever shouts. She never makes you feel stupid. She always listens to you. And she's patient with me. I am the youngest one in my class because I skipped a year. So sometimes I forget to use my indoor voice or to wear my glasses. Miss Colman reminds me nicely.

Another thing I like about Miss Colman is that she's always making Surprising Announcements. For instance, on the

Monday after my weekend at the big house, she said, "Class, I have an announcement."

Miss Colman was smiling, so I knew it would be a good announcement. I looked at Ricky Torres, who was sitting next to me. Ricky and I and another girl (Natalie Springer) all wear glasses. So we all sit in the front row. Ricky and I grinned at each other. Then I turned round and glanced at the back row, where Nancy Dawes and

Hannie were sitting. The three of us grinned, too. (I used to sit with Hannie and Nancy. That was before I got my glasses.)

As I turned to face the front again, I caught Pamela's eye. Pamela Harding is a new girl. I don't like her and she doesn't like me.

I almost stuck my tongue out at Pamela, but I remembered that I should act like other second-graders.

Anyway, Miss Colman began to make her Surprising Announcement.

"Class," she said, "as you know, Hallowe'en is on a Saturday this year. So we'll have a class Hallowe'en party on the Friday afternoon before Hallowe'en."

"Yea!" shouted everyone in my class.

Miss Colman smiled. Then she went on. "We'll have refreshments and you can wear your costumes, of course. We'll play some games, but then we will . . ." Miss Colman paused.

I drew my breath. We will *what*? I wondered.

"We will turn off the overhead light and sit in a circle and tell scary stories. Anyone who wants to may tell a story."

Oh, boy! All around me, people were saying things like, "Cool!" and, "I can't wait!" and, "I know the *best* story!"

Ricky said to me, "I'm going to tell the story about the man whose eyeballs fell out and walked around by themselves."

"That's so gross," I replied.

Ricky just laughed. "Hey! he called to one of his friends. "I'm going to tell the story about the walking eyeballs!"

Well, I knew what scary story *I* was going to tell. I was going to tell the Ben Brewer story, of course. It would be the best of all the scary stories. Miss Colman hadn't said we were going to have a storytelling contest, but I wanted to tell the best story anyway.

"Hey, Karen," called a voice.

I turned round. It was Pamela Harding. Yuck.

"What?" I replied.

"What story are *you* going to tell?" she asked.

"Secret," I said.

"I bet you don't have a story at all."

"I do too. What story are *you* going to tell?"

"Secret." Pamela smiled smugly.

"Then I bet *you* don't have a story."

Pamela's face turned red. "I do, too. And it will be the very best one."

Ha. We would see about that.

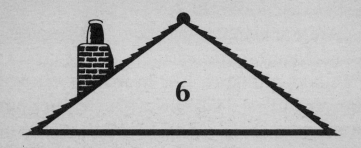

Not-So-Scary Stories

After school that day, Nancy came round to my house. We went to my room and took Emily Junior out of her cage. We let her run around in the special rat playground that Andrew and Seth had made for my seventh birthday.

"Let's try out scary stories," Nancy said to me. "What's the scariest thing that ever happened to you?"

"Getting lost at Disney World," I replied. "But that's not the story I'm going to tell. The story I'm going to tell is a ghost story.

It's much scarier than telling about getting lost at Disney World."

"Are you going to tell about Ben Brewer?" asked Nancy, wide-eyed.

I nodded. Nancy had heard several Ben Brewer stories. They always scared her out of her wits.

"What story are you going to tell?" I asked Nancy.

Nancy frowned.

"You *are* going to tell a story, aren't you?"

"Well, of course," replied Nancy.

I should have known. Nancy loves to be the centre of attention. She wants to be an actress when she grows up.

"Let's see," said Nancy slowly. "Okay. Once — you know my charm bracelet? The one with the horse and all the other animals on it?"

"Yeah."

"Well, once I lost the bracelet. And you know what? A leprechaun had *stolen* it. . . . Honest," she added when she saw my face.

"How do you know?" I asked.

"Because I found it in my underwear drawer, and I *never* keep it there."

"Hmmm," I said.

"Not scary enough?" asked Nancy.

"I don't think so," I replied. "Tell me another."

Nancy told *two* more stories. They weren't scary either.

"Tell me a Ben Brewer story," said Nancy at last.

"Okay." I told Nancy just what I'd told

Hannie on Saturday. I told her all the Ben Brewer stories in one. I told how Ben was haunted by a ghost in his old age, and how he haunts the big house now. Especially the attic and his room on the second floor.

"But *who* was haunting Ben?" Nancy wanted to know.

"I'm not sure."

"And *why* was a ghost haunting Ben? There must have been a reason."

"Yeah. . . . And another thing," I went on. "Why did Ben become a ghost? Hmm, I'd better work on this story."

"Why?" asked Nancy.

"Because I've got to tell the scariest story of all. I have to show Pamela Harding that I know a story and it's a good one."

"Pamela", said Nancy, "is not the only other person who will be listening to your ghost story. And anyway, this isn't a competition."

"I know, I know," I replied. "But I still want a good story. The *best* story. I'm sorry, but I do. And right now, this story isn't finished. We have too many questions about it. I'll have to find out what happened to Ben Brewer and why he was haunted."

"Oh, just make something up," said Nancy.

"No, I think a *true* ghost story will be scarier. Don't you?"

"Yes," Nancy replied, and shivered. She paused. "A true ghost story . . ."

"Ooh," was all I said. I felt a little scared.

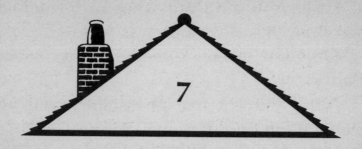

Help From Kristy

After a while, Nancy said she had to go home. We took Emily Junior out of the playground and put her back in her cage. Then Nancy left.

I found Mummy and Andrew in the kitchen. Mummy was making dinner and Andrew was helping. He was stirring something in a bowl at the table. He was standing on a chair, wearing an apron. The apron came down to his feet.

I giggled. He looked funny.

Then I said, "Mummy?"

"Yes?" Mummy turned away from the cooker to look at me.

"Remember when you and Daddy were still married?"

"Yes." Mummy looked a little nervous. Sometimes I ask her to marry Daddy again. She doesn't like to talk about that.

"And you and Daddy and Andrew and I lived in the big house?"

"Yes," said Mummy again.

"Well, when you lived in the big house, did you ever see Ben Brewer's ghost?"

"Karen —" Mummy began.

And then *Andrew* started to look nervous. He stopped his stirring.

"Or do you know anything *about* Ben Brewer?" I went on.

"He was just a lonely old man," Mummy told me.

"No. That's not true," I replied. "I mean, maybe he *was* lonely, but he was haunted by a ghost, too."

"The one that could come down his

chimney?" said Andrew. His eyes had grown huge.

"Yes," I said.

"Karen, those are just stories," Mummy told me.

"How did they start?" I asked. "Huh? How did they start?" I sat at the kitchen table, crossed my arms, and looked at Mummy.

"The way most silly stories start," she answered. She sat down at the table, too, and pulled Andrew onto her lap. "People think someone is a bit odd, so they make up stories about why he's odd. Your great-grandfather was a recluse. Do you know what that means?"

"That he wrecked things?" suggested Andrew.

"No, silly," I said. "*I* know what a recluse is. It's a person who stays inside all the time and won't come out."

"Right," said Mummy. "And that's all that was wrong with Ben Brewer. Except for the fried dandelions. I think that's true, too. And that's as strange as being a recluse. So people made up stories about your poor great-grandfather."

"Are you *sure*?" I asked.

"*Yes*," said Mummy.

"Then why won't Boo-Boo go near the second floor at the big house?" I asked her. I felt pleased with myself.

"Because he's lazy," said Mummy. She put Andrew back on his chair and returned to her cooking.

"No," I said. "It's because he knows about the ghost of old Ben. Animals can sense those things. Boo-Boo is afraid."

"He's a 'fraidy-cat," said Andrew, giggling.

I made a face. "You two aren't taking this seriously. I'm going to phone Kristy," I said. "She'll help me find out the true ghost story. . . . Can I call Kristy?" I asked Mummy.

"Of course," she answered.

I knew that Mummy didn't think Kristy and I would find out anything about Ben Brewer. But *I* knew better.

I phoned the big house. Kristy answered the phone! That was a good sign. I told her what I wanted to do.

"Will you help me?" I asked her.

"Of course," she replied. "Come round tomorrow after school. We'll do some detective work."

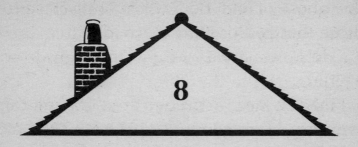

The Mystery Grows

The next afternoon, my big stepbrother Charlie came to the little house to pick me up. He has his own car and he's very proud of it. Then Charlie drove me back to the big house. Kristy met me at the front door.

"Hi!" I cried. "Thank you, Charlie! Okay, Kristy. Let's get to work."

Kristy has as much energy as I do. "Ready when you are," she replied.

The only thing I could think of to do was to look at some old books in the library. Not in the public library. In the room Daddy and Elizabeth *call* the library, where they keep their books. Daddy collects old-fashioned ones. They're so old that their pages are yellow and they smell funny.

"Let's start in the library," I said.

"Okay," agreed Kristy.

We went straight to the oldest of the old books. Some of the books were about Stoneybrook a long time ago. We looked at those first.

"Guess what!" I exclaimed. "They used to spell the name of our town wrong. They spelled it like this: S-t-o-n-e-y-b-r-o-o-k-e. They put an extra 'e' on the end."

"I don't think it was wrong," said Kristy. "That was just the way the name was spelled a long time ago."

"Oh," I said.

Kristy and I looked at the history books. They were hard to read and we couldn't find out anything about my great-grandfather.

Then suddenly Kristy cried, "Hey, look! A genealogy!"

"A what?" I said.

"A genealogy. That's a book that tells about the people in a family. And here is the Brewer genealogy. Old Ben must be in here."

Guess what. He was! We found him towards the back of the book. But we didn't find much information.

"All it says", Kristy told me, "is the date Ben was born; the names of his parents; the date he got married; the name of his wife; when they had Jeremy, their son — he would

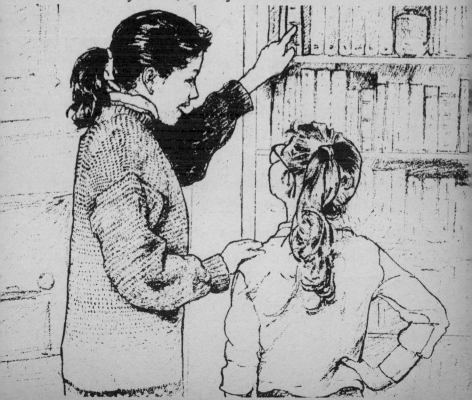

be your grandfather — and the dates when Ben and his wife died."

"That isn't very helpful, is it?" I said.

"No," replied Kristy. She looked disappointed.

"You know what?" I said shakily. "I don't think we're going to find anything here. We're going to have to go into Ben's bedroom."

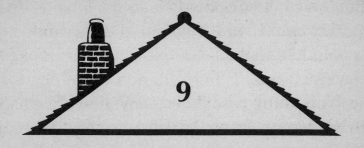

In Ben Brewer's Room

"**I**nto Ben Brewer's *bed*room?" cried Kristy. "Oh, Karen . . ."

"We went in the attic once," I reminded her. "We thought the attic was haunted, but nothing happened. Except that David Michael played a trick on us."

"Yeah," said Kristy, smiling "He hid, and we thought he had disappeared. But nothing bad happened. Still, Ben's bedroom . . ."

We had to go, though. We couldn't think

of any other way to find out more about Ben. Well, I suppose we could have called Daddy at his office, but I didn't think he would like that.

Kristy and I held hands. Bravely we walked to the first floor. Bravely we walked to the second floor. Bravely we walked down the hallway to Ben Brewer's bedroom. We stood in front of the closed door. We didn't feel so brave any more.

"I wish the door was open," said Kristy. "Then we could see inside."

"Maybe it's locked!" I said hopefully.

"Maybe," replied Kristy.

I turned the handle. The door opened easily. "Here goes," I said.

Very, very slowly Kristy and I walked inside the room.

"Phew!" I said. "This place smells."

"It's just musty," said Kristy. "It *has* been shut up for a long time. It's dusty and the air is stale."

We tiptoed around the room. Some of the furniture was covered with sheets. What

wasn't covered looked so, so old. And messy.

"Ben Brewer wasn't very neat, was he?" I said.

"Not at all," agreed Kristy.

There was stuff everywhere — old newspapers, candles, books, clothes, a clock on the mantelpiece over the fireplace.

"You know what I think?" I said. "I think this is exactly the way Ben's room looked when he died. No one has touched it for years and years," I added dramatically.

"Hey," whispered Kristy. "There's the fireplace the ghost came down." (Kristy knew the stories as well as I did.)

Kristy and I peered into the fireplace. It looked like an ordinary old fireplace. The bricks were black from Ben's fires, and it was filled with ashes. That was all.

Kristy and I didn't feel so scared any more. We let go of each other's hands and walked round the room by ourselves. We poked into things. We looked under sheets and on bookcases.

Kristy had just said, "Well, I suppose

there's nothing here," when I let out a scream.

"What? What's the matter?" Kristy ran to my side.

"Look what I found," I said.

It was a book. I'd opened a drawer in a table by Ben's bed. I had seen a tiny knob inside. When I touched it, another drawer — a secret one — had sprung out from the back. And in that drawer was a diary. I opened it. I saw the name Jeremy Brewer. I flipped through the book to see what I could learn, but Jeremy's handwriting was hard to read, so I gave the book to Kristy to look at.

What I had found was the story of Ben Brewer. Or most of it.

"It's here," Kristy whispered. "Ben's son Jeremy kept a diary, and the story is *here*."

Just from reading a few pages, Kristy knew we had found a really spooky story. And the spookiest thing about it was that it was true. It had to be. Diaries are always true . . . aren't they?

I grabbed the book with one hand and Kristy with the other.

We ran all the way downstairs to Kristy's bedroom.

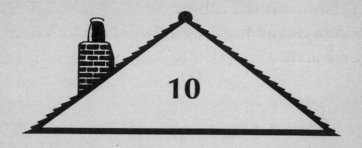

10

Ben's Birthday

"Oh, my gosh. Oh, my gosh," I kept saying as Kristy and I looked through the diary. Sometimes I said, "Ooh, scary."

This is the story we found, the story that Jeremy wrote down about his father, Old Ben Brewer.

Guess what? Ben's birthday was on Hallowe'en. Can you imagine? A Hallowe'en birthday. I wouldn't like that. First of all, you'd probably only get to have one party, a Hallowe'en birthday party, instead of a

Hallowe'en party *and* a birthday party. And second, who'd want to be born on the scariest day of the year?

Then we found out that every ten years, at midnight on Hallowe'en, Ben gives himself a birthday party.

"A *haunted* birthday," I said to Kristy. My teeth began to chatter. That's how scared I was.

"Yeah," said Kristy. She looked nervous.

"Jeremy writes that the birthday parties started *after* his father died."

"What happens at the haunted birthday parties?" I asked Kristy. I was letting her read most of the diary. Jeremy wrote in joined-up writing, and I am not very good at reading that yet. It takes a long time.

"Let me see," said Kristy. She flipped through the book. Then she looked again. "I can't find anything," she said at last. "I would probably have to read the whole diary. From beginning to end. That would take a while."

"I bet that at a haunted birthday party", I said, "Ben invites his ghost friends over and they eat ghost cake. Maybe he invites Morbidda Destiny, too. I wonder if there are other ghosts *in our house* who come to the —"

"Yikes!" shrieked Kristy.

"What?" I asked.

"*This* Hallowe'en, Ben is going to have one of his parties! It's the tenth year. Oh, no. I don't believe it!"

"Are you *sure*?" I asked Kristy.

"Positive." She read to me from the book. She was right.

Suddenly it was my turn to shriek. (Again.) "I'm going to be *here* this Hallowe'en!" I exclaimed. "I'll be at the big house. Hallowe'en is a big-house weekend for Andrew and me. I will be here for a haunted birthday party." I was scared — but I was also excited. My story for the Hallowe'en party was getting better and better, but there were still some things I didn't know.

I didn't know why Ben was haunted when he was alive. I didn't know who had haunted him. I didn't know why he became a ghost after he died. But if I couldn't find out those things, I *could* make them up. I didn't want to, but I could.

Now I knew for sure that my story would be better than Pamela Harding's.

"Do you want to take the diary home with you when your mother picks you up?" Kristy asked me a bit later.

I looked at the diary. It was so spooky. I

almost said, "No." Then I changed my mind.

"Yes," I said. "Maybe if I try very hard, I can read Jeremy Brewer's writing. And if I read the diary carefully, I might find the answers to some of my questions. We didn't read the diary very carefully today."

"No," agreed Kristy. "We didn't."

She handed me the diary. She looked relieved.

Honk, honk! Mummy was here. It was time to go back to the little house.

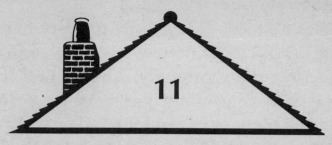

"Haunted Birthday to You"

I thanked Kristy. I called goodbye to Nannie and Charlie and Emily and David Michael. Then I ran outside.

I climbed into Mummy's car and buckled my seat belt. The diary was in my hand. And in that diary was the best story ever.

"What's that?" asked Andrew. He peered over the front seat.

"Oh, just an old diary," I said.

"Whose old diary?" asked Mummy.

"What's a diary?" asked Andrew.

"It's Jeremy Brewer's diary," I told

Mummy. "Ben's son. And", I added, turning
to Andrew, "a diary is a book that you write
in. You tell about things that happen to
you, or things that happen with your family
and friends. It's a very private thing."

"Then how come you've got someone
else's diary?" Andrew wanted to know.

"Because the owner is dead now. He
won't care if I read his diary."

"Karen," said Mummy, "'the owner' is your grandfather. Be nice about him. And how did you get hold of his diary?"

"We found it in Ben Brewer's room. It was in a secret drawer in the table next to his bed. Kristy and I were so sc — I mean, so brave. We marched right into that room and we searched it until we found this diary. Jeremy must have wanted to tell the story of his father. I suppose that's why he put the diary in his father's room. Anyway, did you know that Ben's birthday was on Hallowe'en? And after he died he started giving himself haunted birthday parties."

"Oh, Karen," said Mummy.

"It's true. That's what Jeremy wrote."

"Really?" said Andrew. His bottom lip trembled.

"Really," I told him. "He gives one every ten years. And guess what? *This* Hallowe'en he'll be giving a haunted party and *we* will be at the big house for it. It'll happen at midnight."

Andrew began to cry. "No!" he wailed.

"Then I'm not going to Daddy's for Hallowe'en. I don't want the ghosts to get me."

"Andrew," said Mummy, "there are *no* ghosts. Besides, you'll be asleep at midnight, so you don't need to worry. And Karen, you're scaring your brother. Please stop it right now."

"Okay," I replied. But I sat back in my seat and said softly, "Yup. Every ten years. A haunted party. A haunted birthday party. At midnight."

Mummy stopped the car. She turned around in her seat. "Karen, that's enough. I've just told you that you're scaring Andrew. I don't want to hear another word out of you until we get home. And then I want you to go to your room for fifteen minutes and think about what you've done."

I began to cry. In the front seat, Andrew was crying, too. We cried all the way home. Mummy didn't say anything.

At home, I spent fifteen minutes in my room playing with Emily Junior. I tried to think about what I'd done. But all I could think about was Ben.

When the fifteen minutes was up, Mummy said I could come out. She said it was dinnertime. I ate my whole dinner without saying anything about Ben or Jeremy or the diary.

Mummy gave me a hug and a kiss. I was glad she wasn't cross with me any more. But *I* was cross with *Andrew*. He had got me into trouble because he's a crybaby. So when we were alone I sang to him, *"Haunted birthday to you, haunted birthday to you. Ben Brewer will get you. Haunted birthday to you."*

Do you know what? Andrew stuck his tongue out at me.

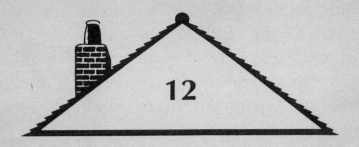

The Wizard of Oz

On a Friday afternoon when there was still a week and a day left before Hallowe'en, Miss Colman let us make decorations for our classroom. We sat wherever we wanted and we made paper pumpkins and witches and skeletons and black cats and ghosts.

Ricky and I took our chairs to the back of the room and sat with Hannie and Nancy. Ricky was making a skeleton. He worked very hard on it. He cut out the arms and legs separately so that they could move. Hannie was making a grinning pumpkin.

She called it a jack-o'-lantern. Nancy was making a black cat. And I was making — what else? — a ghost.

"Well, I've decided what I'm going to be for Hallowe'en," Ricky said. He was busy cutting.

"You have? What?" I asked.

"A petrol pump attendant."

Hannie and Nancy and I glanced at each other.

"Hmm," I said. "Interesting."

"What are you going to be, Karen?" asked Ricky.

"The ghost of Ben Brewer."

We kept on talking about costumes. Suddenly I had a great idea.

"Hey!" I exclaimed, "Ricky, you and Nancy should come trick-or-treating with Hannie and me. We're going out with my brother and my stepbrother and my little sister."

"And Scott," added Hannie.

"Oh, yeah. Your husband," said Ricky.

"But not my brother. Linnie won't go trick-or-treating with any girls."

"You know what else?" I went on. "If we all go together, we should go as characters from a film or something. That would be really cool."

"Yeah!" said the others, except for Hannie.

"Do you think your parents will let you come trick-or-treating in our neighbourhood?" I asked Nancy and Ricky. "My big sister will come with us. Kristy is a babysitter. Your parents wouldn't have to worry."

"I think so," said Nancy and Ricky at the same time.

"Great! Now. What should we dress up as?" I asked.

"How about the kids from Peanuts?" said Nancy. But nobody wanted to be Charlie Brown.

"How about Super-Heroes?" said Ricky.

"Nah," said Hannie.

"I know!" I cried. "*The Wizard of Oz.* We could have a Dorothy and a Tinman and a Wicked Witch of the West and everything. There would be lots of great costumes."

"I want to be the Scarecrow," said Ricky, looking excited.

"I want to be Dorothy," said Nancy. "She's the star."

"Perfect," I said. "I'll be the Wicked Witch of the West. I've already got a witch costume."

"I still want to be a bride," said Hannie.

We talked it over and decided that was okay. Then we thought about who the others could be. This is what we decided: Scott — the Tinman; David Michael — the Lion; Andrew — Toto; and Emily — a Munchkin. We hoped they would like our idea. *We* thought it was great.

But someone else didn't.

"What a stupid plan," said Pamela Harding. She must have been listening. "You lot are such babies. *My* friends and I are going to be waitresses and cheerleaders and punk rockers. We'll be much more grown-up."

"We'll just see about that," I told Pamela. Then I ignored her.

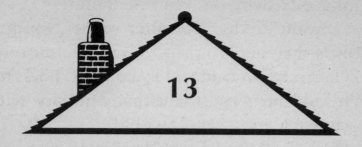

Ruby Slippers

"Three more days! Three more days!" I sang.

It was Wednesday. The next day would be Thursday. That would just be an ordinary day. Then would come Friday, the day of our class Hallowe'en party. And *then* would come . . . Hallowe'en.

Guess what? Everyone liked our idea to go trick-or-treating as characters from *The Wizard of Oz*. No one even wanted to swap costumes. I thought David Michael might say, "I want to be the Tinman, not the raggedy old Lion." But he didn't.

So on Wednesday after school, Mummy was helping Andrew and me with our costumes. My costume was easy. I just had to add some things to my ordinary witch costume so that I would look like the Wicked Witch of the West. But Andrew's costume was hard.

"Toto!" Mummy had exclaimed when I told her what Andrew was going to dress up as. "Where are we going to get a dog costume?"

"Not just a dog costume," Andrew spoke up. "A Toto costume. I have to look like Toto. He is a certain kind of dog."

In the end, Mummy had to make Andrew's costume all by herself. We went shopping. We found material that looked like dark fur. We found a little dog nose. We even found a book that explained how to make whiskers. Andrew's costume was going to be great.

That afternoon Mummy was finishing off

Toto's head. Andrew was helping. He was making the whiskers. I was working on my witch shoes.

When the doorbell rang, I said, "I'll get it! I think it's Nancy. She said she would wear her Dorothy costume round."

I ran to the door and opened it. There stood . . . Dorothy! Nancy looked so much like Dorothy that I gasped. She was wearing a white blouse and a blue-and-white-checked pinafore dress. In her hand was a basket. But best of all, on her feet were pale blue socks and *sparkly ruby slippers!*

"Where did you get ruby slippers?" I asked. I was awed. Nancy wasn't wearing plain old red shoes or even red high heels that belonged to her mother. She had ruby slippers and they fitted her.

"Mummy and Daddy ordered them from a catalogue," she said. "They were a surprise for me. I got them today."

"Come inside and show Andrew and my mother," I said.

So Nancy showed off her costume. Then

she stayed for a while. While she was there, Ricky phoned.

"Guess what? I've got straw for my Scarecrow costume," he said. "I'm going to put it under my hat so that it sticks out."

Then David Michael phoned. "Mum and Watson bought me a *real* Lion costume!" he exclaimed.

Straight after that, Hannie phoned. "Scott's costume is nearly finished," she told me. "He's got a funnel for his hat."

"Great," I said.

"And *I'm* going to carry a bouquet of plastic flowers. That way, they'll last forever. I'm going to be an even more beautiful bride than I was at my wedding."

Ooh, this was so exciting! I couldn't *wait* until Saturday, when our whole group would be together. We were going to have the best costumes in the neighbourhood, even if we did have a bride in the Land of Oz. Maybe no one would notice.

I had almost forgotten about Ben Brewer's haunted birthday party.

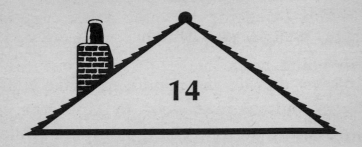

14

Story Time

"Okay, class," said Miss Colman with a big smile on her face. "*Now* you may change into your costumes."

It was Friday. My friends and I had been waiting all day for this moment. Party time! And time to show off our costumes and tell stories.

Waiting had been hard for me. In the morning, I forgot to put up my hand and interrupted people *four times*. At reading I forgot to change to my reading glasses. And

I used my *out*door voice about a million times.

Oh, well. Miss Colman had been very patient.

"Boys," our teacher continued, "take your things and go next door to Mr Berger's classroom. You may change in there while his class is at break. Girls, you stay here and change. I will wait in the hall. Call me if you need any help."

There was a big rush of excitement. When we girls were alone, we scrambled for our costumes. Most of them were in paper bags. I put on my witch outfit quickly. Then came the good part. I had to rub green goo on my hands and face, since the Wicked Witch of the West had green skin. Nancy helped me. (Hannie wouldn't come near me because she didn't want green goo on her white dress.)

Hannie and Nancy and I changed in a corner of the room with our backs to everyone. We kept grinning. We were having so much fun! Nancy waited until the last minute to put on her ruby slippers.

Then we turned round. We planned to show Pamela a thing or two. But Pamela and her friends were ready for us. And just as Pamela had promised, they were wearing grown-up costumes.

Pamela was an airline stewardess. She was wearing a suit (the kind with a skirt) and stockings and even had wings pinned to her jacket. Jannie was dressed up like a punk rocker. She had sprayed her hair blue

and made it all spiky. And she was wearing weird clothes. Leslie was standing with Pamela and Jannie. I knew she was one of the girls in our class who wanted to be cool Pamela's best friend. So I knew she had on a grown-up costume — but I wasn't sure what it was.

"What are you supposed to be?" Nancy asked Leslie.

"A waitress," Leslie replied proudly.

Suddenly I felt silly dressed as a witch. It *was* a baby costume. But then I looked around the room and saw a bunny rabbit and a Raggedy Ann and a princess. I felt better.

The door to our room opened then.

"How are you getting on?" Miss Colman asked us girls.

"We're ready!" I said.

In came the boys. I saw a tramp, a space creature, a cowboy, an Indian, a policeman, some kind of animal, and finally . . . the Scarecrow!

Ricky stood with Hannie and Nancy and

me and we could tell that the other kids were impressed. Except for Pamela, who said, "There's no bride in *The Wizard of Oz*."

When Miss Colman wasn't looking, I made my most horrible face at Pamela.

The party began. Two teacher's aides came in. They brought orange juice and biscuits and crisps. We played two games. And then Miss Colman said, "Okay, storytelling time."

"Miss Colman! Miss Colman!" I cried. "Can I tell my story last?"

I knew I had a *really* good story. I had not found the answers to my questions about Ben, but my story was true – and scary. I wanted to save it and surprise everyone.

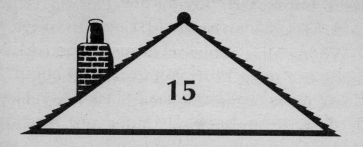

15

The Ghost in
My House

Miss Colman said that I could tell my story last. Whew. I was going to be the hit of the party.

Here is what had happened with my story. I tried reading some more of Jeremy's diary, but it was hard. I could read it, but it took forever. So, maybe the true story of Ben Brewer *was* in the diary. If it was, though, I didn't know it. Since I couldn't find the true story, I'd decided to tell about the haunted birthday parties.

Ricky Torres was the first person to tell a scary story. That was because when Miss Colman said, "Who would like to begin?" Ricky raised his hand really fast. He raised it so high, he practically stood up. And he said, "Ooh, ooh, ooh! Me, me, me!"

He told the story about the walking eyeballs.

Natalie Springer looked as if she was going to throw up.

Five more people told stories. One of them was Pamela. Her story was stupid.

When nobody else had a story to tell, it was my turn. I stood up in front of the class and cleared my throat.

"In my house," I began, "we have a ghost."

Pamela rolled her eyes.

"His name is Ben Brewer, and he was my great-grandfather. His birthday was on . . . Hallowe'en."

Natalie stared at me. She looked terrified.

Pamela yawned.

"Before Ben became a ghost himself," I continued, "he was haunted by *another* ghost."

Pamela looked at her watch. I ignored her.

"Ben Brewer used to be just a normal person," I went on. "When he was young he got married. He and his wife had a baby. It was a boy, and they named him Jeremy. Jeremy was my grandfather."

"This is boring," I heard Pamela whisper to Natalie.

"Then something very sad happened," I said. "Ben's wife died. A few years later, Jeremy got married. So Ben was all alone in our big house. He became a recluse. He never left the house, except to get dandelions, so he could fry them and eat them. Then . . . one rainy night . . . Ben was sitting in his bedroom . . . and the ghost appeared. He came down the chimney. Ben screamed."

(Natalie Springer screamed, too.)

The ghost said to Ben, "I'm going to

haunt you. I'm going to haunt you for the rest of your life."

Pamela was staring at me. She had stopped whispering and fidgeting.

"Finally Ben grew very old, and he died, too," I said. "But he stayed in our house as a ghost. He decided that now he was going to give himself a haunted birthday party. But just once every ten years. He didn't want to overdo things. So you know what happens on his birthday?" I went on. "This clock that never works chimes every hour . . ."

By this time, Pamela was looking very scared.

"And ghosts fly around the second floor, and you can hear the sounds of a party and smell a birthday cake baking."

Natalie began to cry. When she cries, she snorts. And the rest of the kids in my class looked terrified.

Miss Colman said, "Well, Karen. Thank you very much."

I hadn't quite finished, but it was too late.

The bell rang then. And *it* scared *me*. I jumped a mile. Pamela laughed. Still, it had been a very good party. And I had told a very scary story.

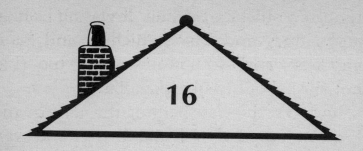

"Trick or Treat!"

That afternoon, as it was growing dark, Mummy drove Andrew and me to the big house. Our Hallowe'en costumes were with us, of course. They were packed carefully in a box.

"Mummy? Do I *have* to go to Daddy's this weekend?" asked Andrew on the way.

"Yup," replied Mummy cheerfully. "We have talked about Karen's ghost story. You know there's nothing to be afraid of."

"I suppose not," said Andrew, frowning.

But the next day, his frowns had gone.

That was because all he could think about was going trick-or-treating. It was all Hannie and Nancy and David Michael and Scott and Ricky and I could think about, too. (I'm not sure about Emily Michelle.)

Just like the day before, the day of the Hallowe'en party, we had to wait and wait and wait to put on our costumes. Kristy had said she would take us trick-or-treating at four o'clock. Around noon, I began looking at my costume. Andrew and David Michael looked at theirs, too. Finally, at two-thirty, we couldn't wait any longer. We got all dressed up. Then Kristy and I dressed Emily. Emily was a very cute Munchkin.

"People will give us *lots* of sweets," said David Michael when he saw her.

At three-thirty, Hannie the bride came round. By a quarter to four, Ricky, Nancy, and Scott had arrived.

"Please can we go now, Kristy?" I begged. "We can't wait another second."

"Okay," said Kristy. But first Daddy and Elizabeth took about a million pictures of

79

us. Then Hannie's parents came round and did the same thing.

When they had finished, my friends and I ran across our front lawn. Our goody bags flopped against our sides.

"Wait for us!" called Kristy. She was holding Emily's hand. Emily's not a fast walker. "Slow down!" Kristy added.

The first house we went to was the house next door. *Not* Morbidda Destiny's — the house on the other side. We rang the bell. Mr Giordano opened the door.

Before any one of us could say a word, Ricky the Scarecrow pushed his way to the front of our group. *"Trick or treat! Smell my feet! Give us something good to eat!"* he sang. *"If you don't —"*

"Ricky!" cried Kristy. "Stop that!"

Ricky stopped. And Mr Giordano smiled. He's nice. He dropped a bar of chocolate into each of our bags.

"See? The song works," said Ricky.

"Well, don't sing it again," Kristy told him. "It isn't polite."

Ricky calmed down. We walked from house to house to house. Almost everyone said what nice costumes we had. Our goody bags grew fuller and heavier.

And everyone *loved* Emily. One lady gave us two chocolate bars each when she saw her. David Michael nudged me. "Told you so," he said.

At last we'd been to every house in our neighbourhood — except Morbidda Destiny's.

"Are we going *there*?" squeaked Andrew, as I started up her drive.

"Of course," I said.

"Why wouldn't we?" asked Ricky.

"It's a witch's house," I told him.

Ricky stopped. Everyone else stopped, too.

"Let's just go home," said Kristy.

"No," I replied. I ran to Morbidda Destiny's front door and rang the bell. No one answered. She wasn't at home. I felt a little disappointed.

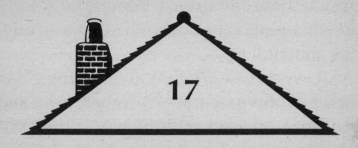

Night Fright

I was sitting on the floor in my room. Trick-or-treating was over for another year. Hannie, Nancy, Ricky and Scott had gone home.

I looked in my goody bag. Then I emptied it out. I counted up the chocolate bars first. Then I counted up the other things I'd got, like packets of peanuts and popcorn. Then I counted up the money. Some people had given us all their change! I had collected quite a lot of money. But the chocolate bars were best.

I wanted to eat a Milky Way. I wanted to eat one badly. (I had got three.) But Daddy and Elizabeth had said, "No sweets until after dinner."

Instead, I took off my witch costume. As I washed the green goo off my hands and face, I thought of something. Ben Brewer.

Tonight would be his haunted birthday party. I'd been so excited about trick-or-treating that I'd forgotten about Ben.

"Ooh," I said, and shivered.

Suddenly I was very, very scared. I left my costume and my sweets (except for one of the Milky Way bars) in a mess on the floor.

I ran downstairs with the Milky Way in my hand.

And I ran straight into Charlie.

"Aaarghhh!" I screamed.

"Karen," said Charlie. "What's wrong? I was just about to call you for dinner. Has Hallowe'en got you spooked?"

"Maybe," I said.

Charlie and I walked to the kitchen together. I sat at the table with my big-house family. When we'd all been served, I said, "Tonight is Ben Brewer's haunted birthday party."

I suppose no one heard me.

Emily said, "Sweets!" loudly, and everyone laughed.

Then Nannie started talking about her bowling team. Sam pinched David Michael under the table. Daddy and Elizabeth kept getting up to answer the door when trick-

or-treaters came. Kristy didn't do anything but eat. She'd been to a dance at school the night before. I think she has a b-o-y-f-r-i-e-n-d.

"Tonight is Ben's haunted party," I said again.

Even Andrew didn't look very worried. "I'll be asleep," was all he said.

I knew that I would be on my own that night. I'd have to protect myself.

The Ghost's Birthday

When I went to bed on Hallowe'en night, I just lay there. I clutched Moosie and Tickly in one arm. I clutched my goody bag in the other arm. Even though I had brushed my teeth, I couldn't help sneaking some chocolate every now and then.

The sweets made me feel better. I could reach into the bag, find something small, like a Wine Gum, and suck on it. The only problem was — then I wondered if I should get up to brush my teeth again.

No, I decided. No way. It was not

midnight yet, but I wasn't going to take any chances. I wouldn't want to run into a stray ghost. Who knew what time Ben's friends would start to arrive for the party?

I don't know when it happened, but at some point I fell asleep.

When I woke up, it was exactly midnight.

I lay in bed as stiff as a board. I could smell a *cake* baking! I could hear people laughing and talking! I think I could even hear horns blowing!

I was too scared to move or make any noise. I just lay in my bed. The next thing I knew, it was morning.

I had lived through a haunted birthday party.

I leapt out of bed. "Hurray!" I shouted. And that was when I saw it. Jeremy Brewer's diary. It was lying on top of my desk. It hadn't been there the night before. When I came to the big house for Hallowe'en, I had asked Daddy to put the diary back in Ben's room. And now it was in *my* room.

I peered at the diary. It was open. And it

was open to some pages that were stuck together. Very carefully, I unstuck them. Kristy couldn't have read these pages.

So I decided to.

I sat on my bed. I read the joined-up writing slowly. (I was getting better at it.) Guess what? Somehow, Jeremy had learned the whole story, the *true* story, about his father. And this is the story:

When Ben was nine years old, he'd had a fight with his best friend, Edward Porter. *Porter?* I thought. *Was Edward someone in Morbidda Destiny's family?* Anyway, during the fight, Ben told Edward that he couldn't come to his tenth birthday party. Right after the fight, Edward disappeared. He was never found. A lot of people thought he had drowned. That made sense, because Jeremy wrote that the ghost who haunted Ben was named Edward and he was always *wet*. (I had never heard that story.) Anyway, Edward haunted Ben because he was angry with him. He still wanted to go to the birthday party. And he told Ben that he would make Ben a ghost after he died.

Finally Ben did die. And Edward kept his promise to Ben. He made him a ghost. And he made him throw a ghost birthday party so that he could go and have fun. Now he makes Ben do that every ten years.

And that's the whole story.

I shivered. What an awful tale. I wanted that diary out of my room. Only this time I would get rid of it myself. I would put it back in Ben's room where it belonged — and I would check for any signs of a ghostly birthday party.

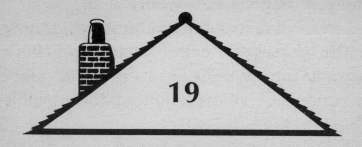

19

Ben Brewer's Clock

I was really scared as I walked up the stairs to the second floor. Below me, I could hear people talking. Nannie and Emily were probably up. So were Daddy and Elizabeth. I wished I could be with them. Instead, I walked down the hall. I stood by Ben's door.

Slowly, I opened it.

I expected to see balloons and cake crumbs and streamers.

But Ben's room looked just like it had

when Kristy and I had explored it. (It felt damp, though.)

I put the diary back in the secret drawer in the table. I was about to stop and check *carefully* for anything — even a little piece of confetti — when I noticed the horrible thing.

The clock on the mantelpiece was *gone*!

The *clock*! When I told my scary story to Miss Colman's class on Friday, I had made up the part about the clock that never worked, except on Ben's birthday.

And now the clock was gone.

I screamed.

Then I raced out of that haunted room and slammed the door behind me. I ran all the way downstairs to the ground floor. I charged into the kitchen. I was out of breath.

Daddy and Elizabeth and Nannie and Emily were there. Emily was in her high chair, eating toast.

"Listen everybody! You won't believe this!" I cried.

"Karen, what's the matter?" Daddy wanted to know. "You look like you've seen a ghost. Try to calm down."

"I didn't *see* any ghosts, Daddy," I said, "but I *heard* them. They've been here. And they had their party last night."

"What are you talking about?" asked Nannie. She sat me down. She put a bowl of cereal in front of me.

"I'm talking about Ben Brewer's haunted birthday party," I said. "I told you about that yesterday. Kristy knows about it, too."

"Oh, Karen," said Daddy with a sigh. (Sometimes I make him sigh.)

"But I smelled a cake baking at *mid*night last night," I said.

"Darling, that was me," said Elizabeth. "I couldn't sleep, so I baked a cake. It's in honour of Emily. She's learned to count to ten."

Emily looked up and smiled. "One, two fee, four, five, sick, seben, eight, nine, ten!" she said proudly.

"But I heard a lot of noise then, too," I went on. "I heard laughing and talking and popping sounds."

"Those were some big kids in the neighbourhood," said Daddy. "They were out late making Hallowe'en mischief."

"Oh." I paused. "Well, there's one more thing. Ben's clock is missing. The one that was on his mantelpiece and didn't work."

"It's working now," said Daddy with a smile. "And it isn't missing. I had it mended. It's in the living room."

"Okay," I said. "How did the diary get back in my room?" I told everyone how I had woken up and found the diary open to the story about Ben and Edward.

Before anyone could say anything, Sam came into the kitchen. He was grinning.

"*You* put the diary in my room last night!" I cried. "Didn't you?"

"What diary?" replied Sam. I could tell that he didn't know what I was talking about. When Sam plays a joke on someone, he likes to brag about it.

Okay, I thought. *Maybe there was no party last night. But where did the diary come from?*

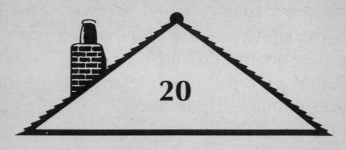

"Is There or Isn't There?"

That afternoon, Nancy's mother drove her over to the big house. Then Nancy and I went to Hannie's. The Three Musketeers were together.

We all had our Hallowe'en chocolate with us, but none of us ate much. We'd eaten a lot of sweets the night before. Especially me.

"Trick-or-treating was fun, wasn't it?" said Hannie.

We were sitting on her back porch. Noodle the poodle was napping in the sun, and Myrtle the turtle was dozing in her box.

"It was brilliant fun," I said. "We should do the same thing next year. Only we should be characters from a different film."

"Yeah," agreed Nancy. "Maybe *The Little Mermaid*."

"How about *One Hundred and One Dalmatians*?" said Hannie, giggling. "We would all be dalmatians! . . . Except me. I think I will be a bride every Hallowe'en. Or as long as Scott and I are married."

"I wonder how Pamela's Hallowe'en was,"

I said. "I wonder if she's too grown-up to go trick-or-treating. Maybe she stays at home and gives out the chocolate. If she does, I'm going to go to her house next year. And I will ring her bell and say, 'Trick or treat. Smell my feet.' And then I really *will* make her smell my feet!"

Hannie and Nancy and I laughed so loudly that we woke up Noodle. He left the porch looking grouchy.

"Well, I have some news," I said. I reached into my goody bag and pulled out a piece of Bazooka bubble gum. I unwrapped it and began chewing.

"What?" asked Hannie and Nancy together.

"I found out the *real* story of Ben Brewer. All of it."

"You *did*?" Hannie looked frightened.

I told my friends what had happened the night before. I told them about smelling the cake and hearing the noises. *Then* I told them about the clock. Of course, they were most interested in the diary and the story.

"How do you think the diary got into your room?" asked Nancy.

She asked it just as Hannie said, "I wonder if Morbidda Destiny is Edward Porter's niece. Or maybe even his younger sister."

"I don't know," I replied. "I don't know about either thing. The diary scares me more, though. I *know* Daddy put it away. And even if he didn't, I know it was *not* next to my bed when I went to sleep last night. And it was so weird. The diary was open to those stuck-together pages that told the story I'd been looking for. Even Kristy didn't find the story. It was almost as if . . . as if Ben Brewer wanted me to know what happened to him."

"Ooh," said Hannie and Nancy.

(I was glad Natalie Springer wasn't there. If she had been, she would have started crying and snorting.)

"I wonder if there really was a haunted party in your house last night," said Nancy.

"I wonder if there really are ghosts in my house," I said.

"I suppose we'll never know," said Hannie.

"Well, at least you won't have to worry about a haunted birthday party for ten more years," Nancy pointed out.

"That's true," I replied. "And I'll be seventeen then. We all will be. Gosh, that's *Charlie's* age! I'll be a grown-up. Almost. Maybe I won't even believe in ghosts any more. Charlie doesn't."

"You just never know," said Hannie again.

THE BABYSITTERS CLUB